my street

written by Rebecca Treays

illustrated by Rachel Wells

digital artwork by Andrew Griffin

geography consultant: Rex Walford

senior designer: Non Figg;   managing designer: Mary Cartwright;
series editor: Felicity Brooks   American editor: Peggy Porter Tierney

restaurant

antique
shop

COMMUNITY CENTER

Bella's Bistro

POST OFFICE

Granny's Attic

There are lots of different kinds of buildings in my street, from a post office to a retirement home. What kinds of buildings are there in your street?

gas
station

GARY'S GAS

This is my street. It is the longest street in my town.

This is the street where my friend Jack lives. His street is a cul-de-sac. This means it doesn't go anywhere.

The street is wider at this end, so cars can turn around.

There is a bench in my street where tired people can sit down. Trash cans and lampposts make the street cleaner and safer. How many trash cans can you spot?

Look at my street with the flaps shut again. Then open them and see what differences you can spot.

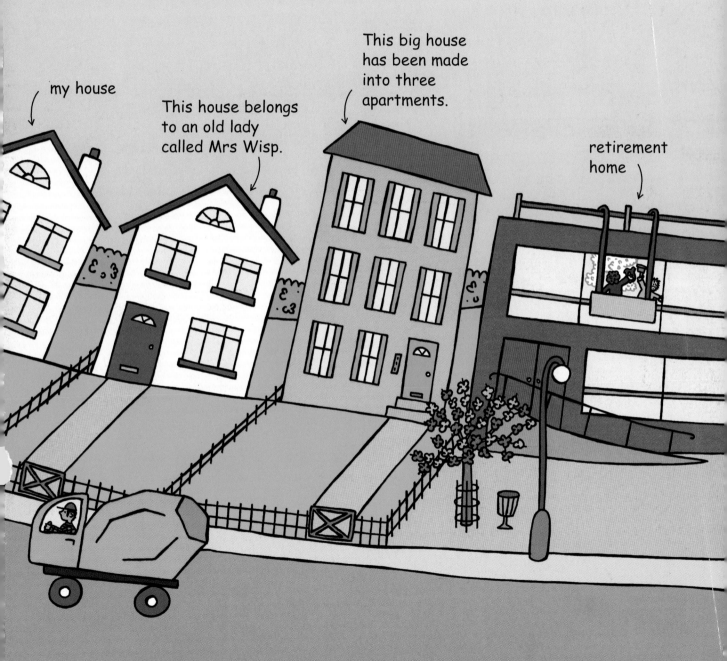

my house

This house belongs to an old lady called Mrs Wisp.

This big house has been made into three apartments.

retirement home

Lift the flaps to see more of my street.

This is my house. I live here with my mom, dad and granny.

The walls of my house are made of bricks. Bricks are made of a type of soil called clay.

Dad is fixing some shingles.

Windows are made of glass, which lets in light.

Window-ledges are made of wood.

Bricks and glass keep the wind and rain out of my house.

The letterbox is metal.

Granny

These floor plans show the rooms in my house as if you were looking down on them from above. They just show the floors and the top of the furniture.

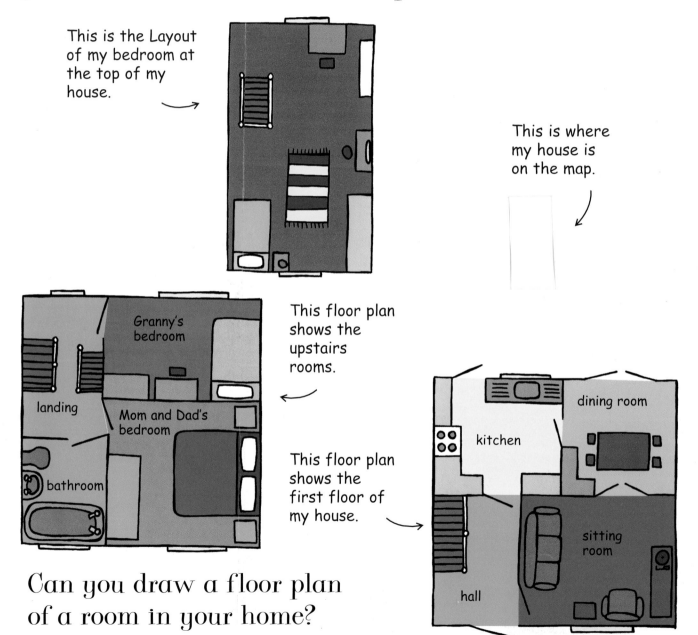

This is the Layout of my bedroom at the top of my house.

This is where my house is on the map.

This floor plan shows the upstairs rooms.

Granny's bedroom

landing

Mom and Dad's bedroom

bathroom

This floor plan shows the first floor of my house.

kitchen

dining room

sitting room

hall

Can you draw a floor plan of a room in your home?

Jack's street is much quieter than mine because cars can't drive down it on their way to somewhere else. It is safer to ride our bikes here.

Jack's house

Jack's dad

Jack's mom

Jack's cat, Slinky

Jack's big brother

me

Jack

Is your street busy? Count how many cars pass your home in five minutes.

If you took the front off my house, this is what you would see.

My bedroom is all the way at the top of my house. It has a sloping ceiling.

bathroom

Mom and Dad's bedroom

sitting room

Mom

hall

All over the world, people make their homes of different things. What is yours made of?

African houses stay cool in the hot sun.

Many African homes have mud walls and roofs made of grasses.

Floating homes are sometimes built from reeds.

houseboat

Some people live on houseboats on rivers and lakes.

Tents can fold up into small bundles.

Some people live in tents which they carry around with them.

Jack and I would like to live in our very own tree-house.

Under my street there are lots of pipes and tunnels. You can't see them, but there are clues that they are there.

↑ This metal plate on the wall means that there is a big underground water pipe nearby.

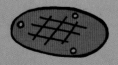 Under these round metal covers are manholes. Manholes are spaces which people can climb into to check on underground pipes and cables.

Lift the flaps to see what's under my street.

Some telephone messages travel from telephones through underground cables.

Rainwater falls through these grates and is carried away by underground pipes. This stops my street flooding when it rains.

Lots of different kinds of vehicles come down my street. Where do you think all these are going?

Can you match them up with these places?

Can you spot Jack and me dancing?

The party goes on until after dark.

Every summer we have a big party in my street.
The road is closed to all traffic.

There are lots of things to prepare.

There will be a lot of cleaning up to do tomorrow!

Everyone has a fantastic time.

Mrs. Wisp has some old photos which her grandmother gave her. They show my street about 100 years ago.

This is a lamplighter. He used a long pole with a hook to turn on the gas and light the street lights.

This woman is a peddler. She traveled around selling things from her basket.

This is a bus. It was a big carriage pulled by horses. This was its first journey along my street.

This is Mrs. Wisp's mom and uncle. Look at their toys. Do you have any toys like this?

Most of the old houses and shops from 100 years ago aren't here anymore. These old shops stood where the Mini-mart is today.

Some people are up really early in my street...

COMMUNITY CENTER

Bella's Bistro

The mail carrier delivers letters.

Mrs. Dawn is on her way to bed. She works all night at the gas station.

Mrs. Mutt walks her dog before she goes to work.

Street cleaners clean up the litter and leaves.

Sun Clean

Mr. Grey drives to his office in Smogton.

What time does everyone get up in your home?

and there are still things going on long after I'm in bed.

COMMUNITY CENTER

Bella's Bistro

Pedro's Plumbing

Goodnight bus

A police officer is on duty all night.

Mrs. Dawn is off to work.

Mrs. Mutt is giving her dog a last walk.

These people are on their way home. They have had a night out in Smogton.

The plumber is on his way to an emergency. There is a leaky pipe in Jack's house.

I'm always visiting the stores in my street. I go to the post office to send letters to my pen pal, Carlos, who lives in South America.

These people have come miles to buy antiques.

I just like to look in the window of the antique store. It is full of expensive old things. My favorite is a wooden rocking horse. Dad says it is 150 years old.

Mini-mart sells all kinds of different things.
I sometimes spend my allowance here. Lift the flap to
see what you can buy inside.

This is my shopping list. Can you spot all these things in the Mini-mart?

birthday card
wrapping paper
frozen peas
box of cereal
orange fizzo drink
2 jam tarts
4 juicy oranges

treat from the
penny basket

Streets and roads are named after different things. Some of the streets in my town are named after famous people.

Glenda Macdougal lived about 150 years ago. She is famous because she wrote lots of storybooks about a family of badgers.

Harry Porter opened a school in my town about 100 years ago. Jack and I go to that school now.

Other streets are named after where they were built.

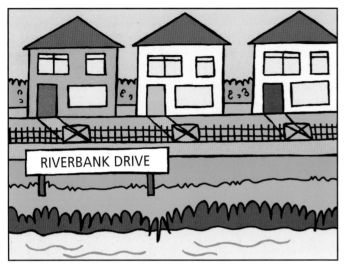

This street is beside the river.

This one is on the top of a hill.

This street is named after where it leads to.

Why do you think this street is named Blossom Lane?

How do you think your street got its name?

Most people don't live in the same house all their lives. Our next-door neighbor, Mrs. Wisp, is moving out. She is going to live with her sister.